HOW TO BE A
Good Dog

dedicated to my mother, Jessie Page

HOW TO BE A
Good Dog

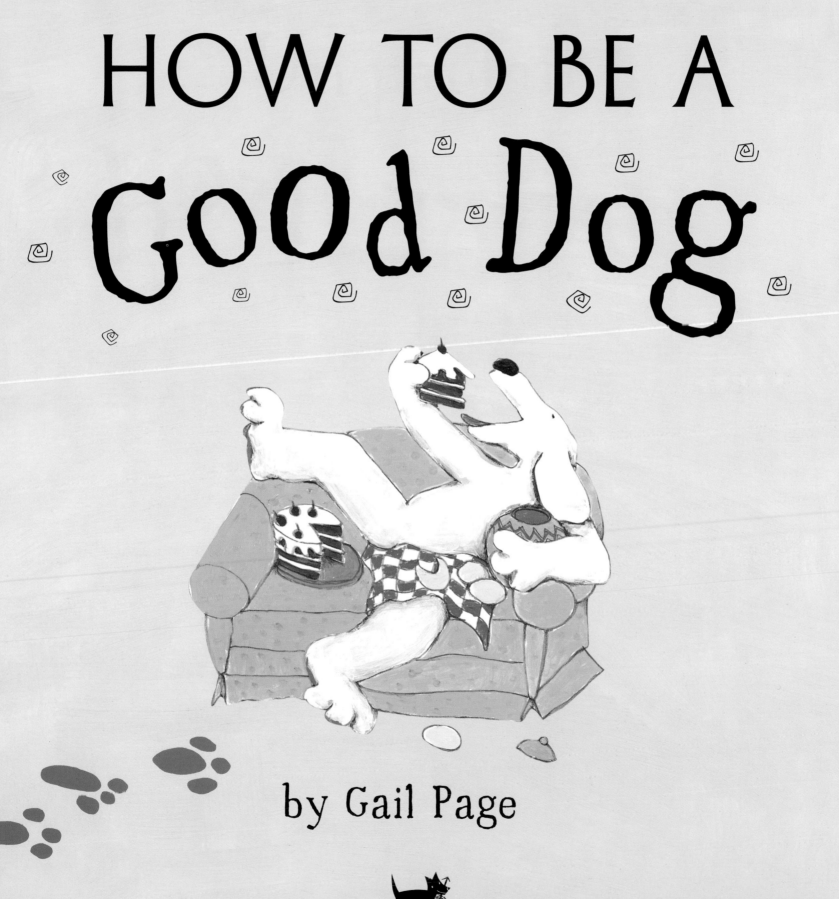

by Gail Page

BLOOMSBURY
CHILDREN'S
BOOKS

Bobo tried hard to be a good dog.

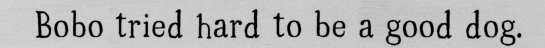

He loved to hear Mrs. Birdhead say,

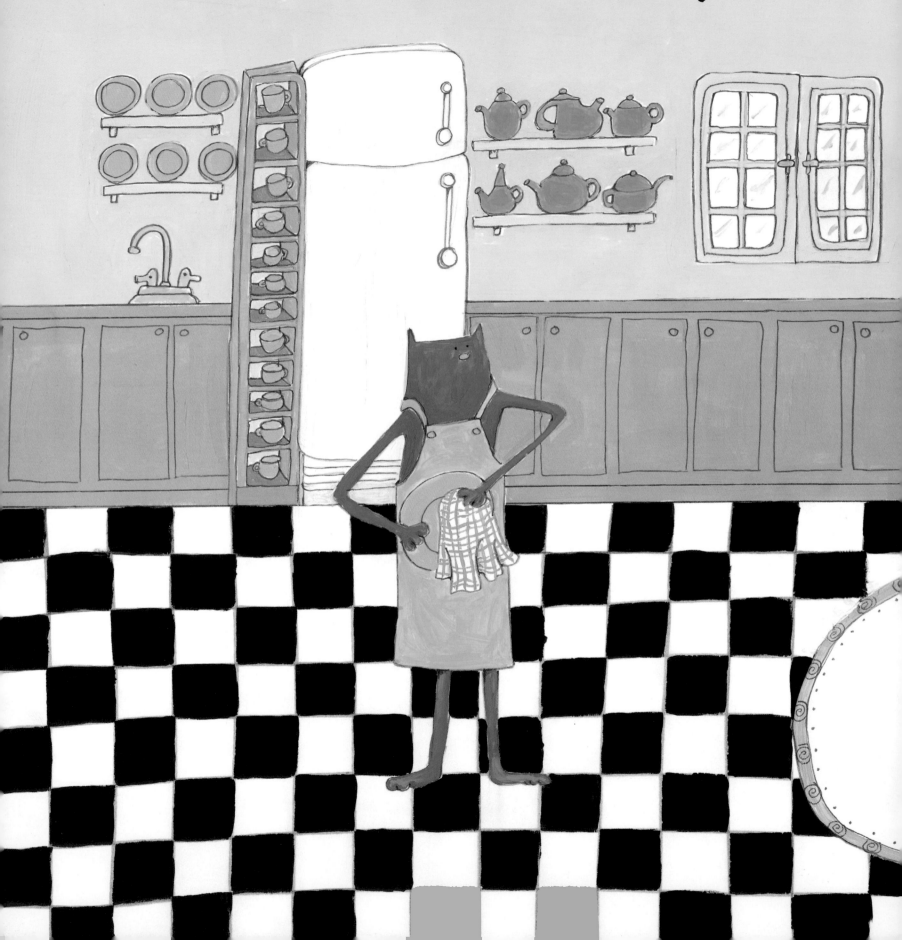

But being good was sometimes
very difficult.

bark bark bark bark

And when Bobo was a bad dog,
Mrs. Birdhead got strict!

Bobo missed Mrs. Birdhead.
He even missed Cat.

And much to Cat's surprise,

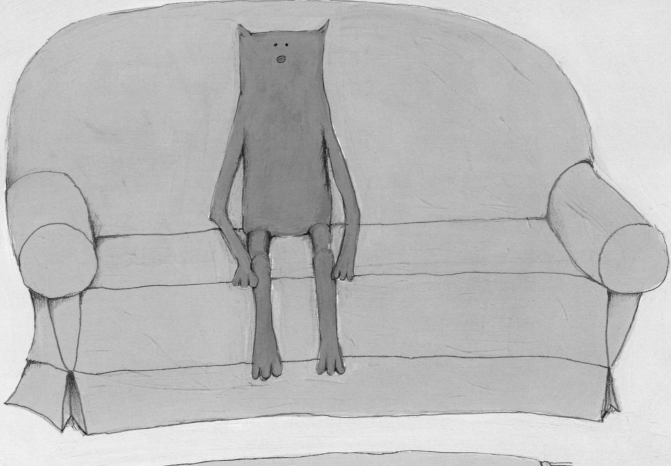

she missed Bobo.

How could she get him
back into the house?

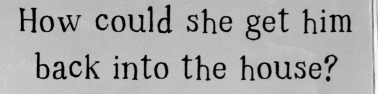

"With a few easy commands,
you can teach your dog
to be good," the book said.

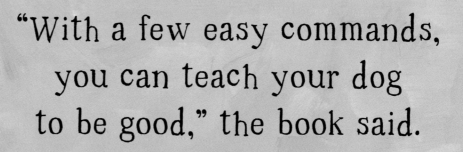

When Mrs. Birdhead went
out to run errands, Cat gave
Bobo his first lesson.

They began with SHAKE.

It went very well.

Next was FETCH.

Oops!
Bobo missed.

Luckily, the window
was open.

HEEL turned out
to be very handy.

Then it was time to practice **SIT**.

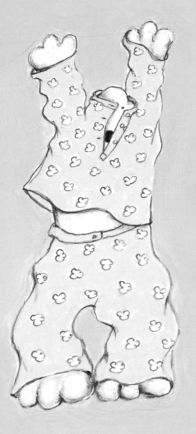

LIE DOWN was next.
It came naturally to Bobo.

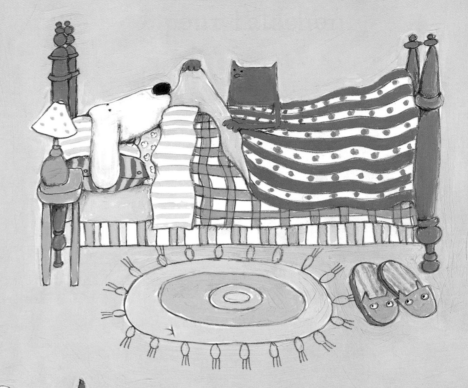

ROLL OVER
was a bit harder.

But STAY was the
easiest command of all.

Well, it was easy until...

...Mrs. Birdhead came home with
the groceries!

Cat tried to control Bobo.

HEEL!

But nothing worked.
Bobo couldn't wait to show
Mrs. Birdhead everything he had learned.

But before Mrs. Birdhead
could get mad, Bobo showed
her how he could:

SHAKE!

SIT!

LIE DOWN!

ROLL OVER!

HEEL!

FETCH!

And when Mrs. Birdhead
told him he was a good dog,

Bobo STAYED, and STAYED, and STAYED.

the end

Art created with acrylics
Typeset in McKracken
Book design by Lizzy Bromley

Published by Bloomsbury Publishing, New York, London, and Berlin
Distributed to the trade by Holtzbrinck Publishers

Library of Congress Cataloging-in-Publication Data
Page, Gail.
How to be a good dog / by Gail Page.
p.   cm.
Summary: Cat helps Bobo the dog show Mrs. Birdhead how good he is.
ISBN-10: 1-58234-683-6 · ISBN-13: 978-1-58234-683-0
[1. Dogs—Fiction. 2. Cats—Fiction.] I. Title.
PZ7.P1377 How 2006   [E]—dc22   2005057012

First U.S. Edition 2006
Printed in China
6 8 10 9 7 5

Bloomsbury Publishing, Children's Books, U.S.A.
175 Fifth Avenue, New York, NY 10010

All papers used by Bloomsbury Publishing are natural, recyclable products
made from wood grown in well-managed forests. The manufacturing processes
conform to the environmental regulations of the country of origin.